Around the World

Life and Culture in
SUB-SAHARAN
AFRICA

TAMRA B. ORR
AND
JILL KEPPELER

Published in 2021 by The Rosen Publishing Group, Inc.
29 East 21st Street, New York, NY 10010

Copyright © 2021 by The Rosen Publishing Group, Inc.

All rights reserved. No part of this book may be reproduced in any form without permission in writing from the publisher, except by a reviewer.

First Edition

Editor: Siyavush Saidian
Book Design: Seth Hughes

Photo Credits: Cover Shutterstock.com/Marisha_SL; p. 5 YASUYOSHI CHIBA/Contributor/AFP/Getty Images; p. 7 Shutterstock.com/Peter Hermes Furian; p. 8 REDA&CO/Contributor/Universal Images Group/Getty Images; p. 9 Eric LAFFORGUE/Contributor/Gamma-Rapho/Getty Images; p. 10 © iStockphoto/HomoCosmicos; p. 11 (top) Per-Anders Pettersson/Contributor/Getty Images News/Getty Images; p. 11 (bottom) © iStockphoto/peeterv; p. 14 (top) RAJESH JANTILAL/Stringer/AFP/Getty Images; p. 14 (bottom) TONY KARUMBA/Contributor/AFP/Getty Images; p. 17 Michel HUET/Contributor/Gamma-Rapho/Getty Images; p. 18 Eamonn McCabe/Popperfoto/Contributor/Popperfoto/Getty Images; p. 19 (top) JEKESAI NJIKIZANA/Contributor/AFP/Getty Images; p. 19 (bottom) Shakko/Wikimedia Commons; p. 20 Eric Lafforgue/Art in All of Us/Contributor/Corbis News/Getty Images; p. 23 EDUARDO SOTERAS/Contributor/AFP/Getty Images; p. 24 (top) AFP Contributor/Contributor/AFP/Getty Images; p. 24 (bottom) Neil Thomas/Contributor/Corbis News/Getty Images; p. 26 Eric Lafforgue/Art in All of Us/Contributor/Corbis News/Getty Images; p. 28 (left) DE AGOSTINI PICTURE LIBRARY/Contributor/De Agostini/Getty Images; p. 28 (right) Eric Lafforgue/Art in All of Us/Contributor/Corbis News/Getty Images; p. 29 OZAN KOSE/Contributor /AFP/Getty Images; p. 30 (left) Michael Bowles/Stringer/Getty Images Entertainment/Getty Images; p. 30 (right) ADRIAN DENNIS/Staff /AFP/Getty Images; p. 31 Christian Science Monitor/Contributor/Christian Science Monitor/Getty Images; p. 34 CARL DE SOUZA/Staff /AFP/Getty Images; p. 35 CELLOU BINANI/Stringer Editorial/Getty Images; p. 36 Patricia Lanza / Contributor/Archive Photos/Getty Images; p. 37 DE AGOSTINI PICTURE LIBRARY/Contributor/De Agostini/Getty Images; p. 38 PIUS UTOMI EKPEI/Contributor/AFP/Getty Images; p. 39 RAJESH JANTILAL/Contributor/AFP/Getty Images; p. 41 SEYLLOU DIALLO/Stringer Editorial/AFP/Getty Images; p. 42 CRISTINA ALDEHUELA/Contributor/AFP/Getty Images; p. 43 DEA/F. GALARDI/Contributor/De Agostini/Getty Images; p. 44 Eric Lafforgue/Art in All of Us/Contributor/Corbis News/Getty Images; p. 45 (left) STEPHANE DE SAKUTIN/Staff/AFP/Getty Images; p. 45 (right) picture alliance/Contributor/picture alliance/Getty Images.

Cataloging-in-Publication Data
Names: Orr, Tamra B. and Jill Keppeler
Title: Life and culture in Sub-Saharan Africa / Tamra B. Orr and Jill Keppeler
Description: New York : PowerKids Press, 2021. | Series: People around the world | Includes glossary and index.
Identifiers: ISBN 9781725321724 (pbk.) | ISBN 9781725321748 (library bound) | ISBN 9781725321731 (6 pack) | ISBN 9781725321755 (ebook)
Subjects: LCSH: Africa, Sub-Saharan–Social life and customs–Juvenile literature. | Africa, Sub-Saharan–Juvenile literature.
Classification: LCC DT351.O77 2021 | DDC 967–dc23

Manufactured in the United States of America

CPSIA Compliance Information: Batch #CSPK20: For Further Information contact Rosen Publishing, New York, New York at 1-800-237-9932

Contents

Introduction 4
Differences and Similarities

Chapter 1 6
A Land of Diversity

Chapter 2 13
Language and Literature

Chapter 3 20
Beliefs Old and New

Chapter 4 27
Works of Art

Chapter 5 33
Music, Dance, and Stories

Chapter 6 40
Challenges, Victories, and Life

Glossary 46

For More Information 47

Index 48

Introduction
DIFFERENCES AND SIMILARITIES

The continent of Africa is huge, with **diverse** landscapes and peoples. Located in the northern part of the continent is the world's largest hot desert, the Sahara. This sprawling desert covers more than 3.3 million square miles (8.6 million sq km), and it keeps expanding every year. South of this desert is the region known as sub-Saharan Africa. This section of Africa is huge on its own. In fact, the United States, China, and India could all fit inside its borders, with some room left over.

Sub-Saharan Africa is made up of 46 countries, according to the United Nations. Spread throughout these countries and islands are more than 1 billion people. While they

diverse: Different or varied.

People dance and sing at a music festival in February 2019 in Tanzania. Sub-Saharan Africa has a rich musical tradition.

share a life in sub-Saharan Africa, they're all different from each other. They speak different languages, they struggle with different issues, and they celebrate life differently.

However, people in many parts of the region deal with similar challenges and concerns, too, including issues of **climate change** (including **desertification**) and access to resources. Despite the challenges of the region, there's a very long, rich history and cultural background found in sub-Saharan Africa, with incredible artistic and musical traditions, vibrant stories, and unique foods and recreation.

desertification: The process where fertile land turns into desert, usually caused by overgrazing.

1 A LAND OF DIVERSITY

Although some people treat sub-Saharan Africa as one single area with a single culture, life is actually very different in different areas. Some people live in traditional villages, some live in very modern cities, and many experience life at varying degrees in between. The peoples of sub-Saharan Africa are very diverse as well. There are more than 3,000 **ethnic** groups living on the African continent. These peoples vary in typical appearance, culture, and many other aspects of everyday life. There's not one overall African culture or group.

CULTURAL CONNECTIONS

Some people don't like the term "sub-Saharan Africa." Although the countries of the region are very different, they all get lumped in together. Many people are trying to get away from this idea.

ethnic: Having to do with a group that shares common cultural traits, such as language.

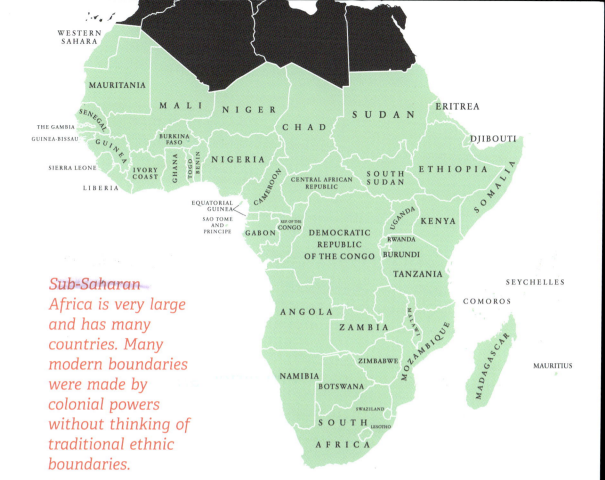

Sub-Saharan Africa is very large and has many countries. Many modern boundaries were made by colonial powers without thinking of traditional ethnic boundaries.

Bantu peoples are **indigenous** to sub-Saharan Africa. They make up several hundred groups in the region, all of which speak languages in the same family. Even within this group, cultures are very diverse, although they may have a common origin. Bantu peoples include the Zulu, Kongo, and Swahili. They live across much of the southern part of Africa. Zambia alone has 72 different Bantu groups. Many Bantu peoples live in villages, while some are **nomadic**.

indigenous: Describing groups that are native to a particular region.

African Architecture

As with many other aspects of the region, architecture in Africa varies widely. People often think of African buildings mostly as simple huts, but while those certainly exist, there are also beautiful religious buildings made of traditional materials and stylish modern structures. Bet Medhane Alem in Ethiopia is said to be the largest rock-hewn, or carved rock, church in the world. It was built in the 13th century and is surrounded by 34 towering columns. Mali has **intricately** designed mosques made of sun-dried mud. In newer architecture, builders are creating a wide variety of structures, some combining both traditional materials and newer, **sustainable**, and lightweight ones.

The rock-hewn churches of Lalibela, Ethiopia, are among the largest **monolithic** structures in the world.

architecture: A method or style of building.

The Yoruba people of west Africa make up the largest ethnic group in sub-Saharan Africa. There are about 20 million Yoruba spread across Nigeria, Benin, and Togo. The Hausa, Igbo, and Oromo peoples are other large groups. Berber peoples mostly live in North Africa, but some also live in Mauritania, Mali, and Niger. The San people of southern Africa are one of the oldest ethnic groups in the world. There are about 100,000 members of this hunter-gatherer people living in Botswana, Namibia, Angola, and other countries in southern Africa.

A group of San women walk in the bush, or wilderness, in Namibia. The San people are one of the oldest in the world and have developed amazing skills for surviving in a harsh environment.

This photograph shows a traditional Konso village in Ethiopia. Homes are made out of old-style materials, such as sticks and grasses for thatched roofs.

There are many small, rural villages in sub-Saharan Africa, but there are also huge cities. In fact, Africa may be the fastest-**urbanizing** continent in the world, with increasing amounts of technology. Lagos in Nigeria, on the Atlantic coast, is the region's largest city. About 21 million people live there. The city of Kinshasa in the Democratic Republic of the Congo is home to about 13.3 million people.

CULTURAL CONNECTIONS

By 2050, experts say sub-Saharan Africa will be home to all 10 countries with the youngest populations in the world.

While some people tend to think of Africans as living only in rural, traditional villages, many people live in houses and apartment buildings.

The city of Lagos in Nigeria looks like many of the large cities around the world, with skyscrapers, traffic, and busy crowds of shoppers.

Dealing with Problems

Life in sub-Saharan also means dealing with certain widespread issues. One of the biggest issues facing the region is weak **infrastructure**. This means that its most important public utilities—such as water, electricity, and road systems—aren't always able to provide the resources that people need. For example, even in Ethiopia, which has one of the region's most developed economies, only 34.3 percent of the roads are paved. Electricity shortages are also a widespread problem. The 10 countries that produce the least electricity worldwide are all in sub-Saharan Africa. There are also issues with access to health care and, sometimes, education.

As of the late 2010s, sub-Saharan Africa had the lowest level of internet use in the world. However, 8 of the 10 countries with the youngest populations in the world are in the region. Technology usage is likely to increase as this younger population grows up.

infrastructure: The equipment and structures needed for a country, state, or region to function properly.

2 LANGUAGE AND LITERATURE

With more than 40 countries, more than 3,000 ethnic groups, and more than 1 billion people, it's no surprise that people in sub-Saharan Africa speak more than 2,100 different languages. In Nigeria alone, people use more than 500 languages. Some of the most widely spoken languages throughout the region are Hausa, Yoruba, Ibo, Swahili, Lingala, and Zulu. However, many people also speak languages brought to Africa through **colonization**, including French and English. Many people speak Arabic, although that language is more concentrated in North Africa. Most Africans speak more than one language.

---

colonization: The act of making or establishing a settlement in a new territory that maintains ties to a distant parent state.

A woman reads a Zulu language newspaper in South Africa. Publications written in the language are on the rise.

Many of the publications in sub-Saharan Africa are written in English, like this one in Nairobi.

The diversity of languages leads to a problem: which language should be used for official communication or any type of written material? Governments face a problem in choosing which languages to use. Declaring an official language is challenging for some countries in sub-Saharan Africa. Doing so could make one or more groups feel insulted and ignored.

Colonization

In the 1800s and 1900s, Europeans colonized many parts of Africa. Great Britain, France, Portugal, Germany, Belgium, Italy, and Spain all established colonies on the continent. This had a major influence on the region that continues today, even after the end of the colonial era. Many countries have official languages that are spoken due to colonization, such as Portuguese in Angola and Cape Verde, French in Benin and Madagascar, and English in Ghana and Nigeria. Also because of colonization, the most-known works of literature from Africa tend to be those written in European languages.

However, when countries officially use languages that many people speak, in time, fewer people speak other languages. Many smaller, local languages used in the region have no written history or record. They'll begin to die out if they don't have living speakers.

CULTURAL CONNECTIONS

The topic of **apartheid** has been featured in many literary works by South African authors. One famous example is *Cry, the Beloved Country* by Alan Paton.

African literature can include written works in both African languages and languages introduced to the region through colonization. It also includes works that come from the region's rich **oral** traditions. Some more modern African literature shows both the effects of colonization and the lasting influences of older storytelling traditions.

A griot is a combination of musician, storyteller, and historian in west Africa. This

CULTURAL CONNECTIONS

Mory Kanté, a griot from Guinea, is a famous artist in west Africa who also had a successful international career. He mixed traditional west African music with R & B and soul music, and his hit song "Yé ké yé ké" was played throughout Europe in the late 1980s.

apartheid: A system of legal racial segregation that existed in South Africa, under which the rights of the majority "non-white" inhabitants of the country were restricted.

hereditary role has been part of the culture in the region for a very long time. Griots preserve the stories and history of their people.

This photo from 1960 shows a traditional griot in Côte d'Ivoire, Africa.

African Authors

Many of the best-known works of literature by African writers were published after World War II. *Things Fall Apart* by Nigerian author Chinua Achebe was published in 1958 and has been called the world's most widely read African novel. In 1986, Wole Soyinka, a member of the Yoruba people, won the Nobel Prize for Literature, an honor that's also gone to Nadine Gordimer of South Africa (1991) and J. M. Coetzee of South Africa (2003). Other notable authors include Chimamanda Ngozi Adichie of Nigeria (*Purple Hibiscus*) and Ngugi wa Thiong'o of Kenya (*Devil on the Cross*).

Author Chinua Achebe is shown in 2009. Achebe died in 2013.

In 2018, storyteller Hatifari Munongi tells folktales to young students visiting a replica of a traditional house outside her home in the city of Harare, Zimbabwe.

African oral literature can include folktales and stories, songs and theater, even riddles and **proverbs**. These things can share the history of the people to whom they belong or teach lessons. African heroic **epics** are a part of the region's oral literature. One example of this form is the Sunjata epic, which tells the tale of Sunjata, a king of Mali during the 13th century.

Older written African literature includes the *Kebra Negast* in the Ge'ez language, which dates to 1300s Ethiopia. Other works were written in Hausa, Zulu, and other languages.

These illustrations are from a copy of the *Kebra Negast*, or *The Glory of the Kings*. This epic from the 14th century is very important to Christians in Ethiopia.

proverb: A short saying that gives advice or expresses a belief.
epic: A long poem that tells the story of a hero's adventures.

3 BELIEFS OLD AND NEW

The mix of religious beliefs in sub-Saharan Africa has changed a great deal over the last 120 years. In 1900, most of the people in the region still followed traditional African faiths. By 2010, however, the number of Christians in the region had soared, from about 7 million to about 470 million, as did the number of Muslims, from about 11 million to about 234 million.

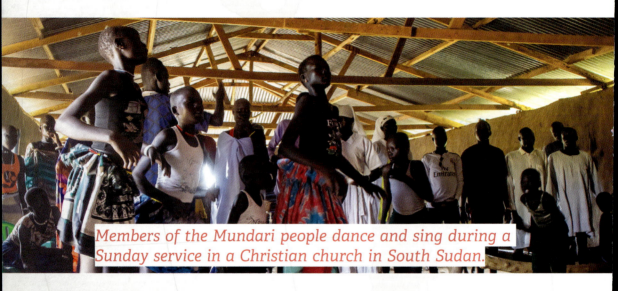

Members of the Mundari people dance and sing during a Sunday service in a Christian church in South Sudan.

By 2015, about 26 percent of the world's Christians lived in the region, as did 16 percent of the world's Muslims. By 2060, researchers say, more than 40 percent of Christians will live in sub-Saharan Africa, as well as 27 percent of Muslims. This increase is driven by a number of factors, including the relatively young age of both Christians and Muslims in the region and a tendency to have more children than Christians and Muslims elsewhere in the world.

CULTURAL CONNECTIONS

Today, there are a number of forms of Christianity in sub-Saharan Africa, including the Catholic, Protestant, Anglican, and Orthodox faiths. Pentecostal churches have grown as well.

Christianity arrived in sub-Saharan Africa first, in the very early days of the church. This was mostly in North Africa, although it did spread to Ethiopia, becoming that kingdom's official religion in the fourth century AD. It started reaching the rest of the region with the

Holidays

Christians and Muslims in sub-Saharan Africa celebrate the same religious holidays members of these religions celebrate elsewhere. Holidays such as Christmas and Easter may be celebrated as **secular** holidays in mostly Muslim countries as well. In fact, sometimes Christians and Muslims choose to unofficially celebrate each other's holidays in a spirit of religious acceptance. Coptic Christians in Ethiopia celebrate Christmas according to their own calendar, so it falls on what would be January 7 in the United States and many other places. Christmas dinner and church services are often part of the festivities in African countries.

A woman walks near a shop selling Christmas decorations in 2020 in Ethiopia. Western-style Christmas decorations are becoming more common in the region.

arrival of the Portuguese in the 1400s, followed by the Dutch, and then spread farther through **missionaries**. Islam reached below the Sahara through trade and with Muslim **refugees** leaving the Arabian Peninsula around the seventh century AD.

secular: Not religious.
refugee: A migrant person who flees their homeland to escape disaster, persecution, or war.

Children sit next to their father at a mosque during the Muslim Eid al-Adha celebrations in Nigeria.

About one-quarter of the people living in Kenya are Roman Catholic.

> ### CULTURAL CONNECTIONS
> The COVID-19 global pandemic, which started in 2019, challenged the health, daily lives, religious customs, and celebrations of people in this region and the wider world.

Religion plays a very strong role in people's everyday lives in the region, with much free time taken up by church activities. Most people attend worship services at least once a week, pray every day (or five times a day in the case of Muslims), and give money to their respective religious institutions or places of worship. They may also take part in religious fasting, such as during Muslim Ramadan or Christian Lent.

Traditional Religions

Indigenous African beliefs vary widely throughout the region and between ethnic groups, but there are often common themes. These religions often have a supreme being who created and ordered the world, as well as lesser spirits. There's no formal text such as the Bible or Qur'an, but there are many oral traditions. Ritual acts, sacred objects, and ancestors in the spirit world are very important. These ancestors are often believed to be go-betweens for the living and the gods. These beliefs are often less religious and more basic ways of life, not separated from other aspects.

However, while many residents of sub-Saharan Africa identify as Christian or Muslim, many also believe in more traditional religious elements alongside those religions. Some keep a belief in sacrifices to ancestors and spirits or in the power of charms and **amulets**. Many people still turn to religious healers when they or others are sick. They share traditional ideas and beliefs through storytelling, rituals, songs, and art.

Women dance during a ceremony in 2019 in Côte d'Ivoire (Ivory Coast), Africa.

4 WORKS OF ART

There's an enormous variety of visual art forms native to sub-Saharan Africa, and they're an important part of the region's cultures. Just like in any other region, some of this art has religious or ritual importance, while some is simply created for entertainment or **aesthetic** reasons. Often, certain objects have meaning because of how they're used in combination with performance arts such as dance and music.

Masks are a well-known and significant aspect of traditional sub-Saharan African art. Different peoples created and used masks in different ways, and they remain a popular and meaningful art form today. They may be carved from wood or made of metals, leather, clay, or other materials. People may use masks during festivals, dances, and ceremonies. Some groups, including some peoples of the Democratic Republic of the Congo, may use them for **initiation** rituals. The Northern Igbo people create colorful cloth *ijele* masks that may be 12 feet (3.7 m) high and 6 feet (1.8 m) around.

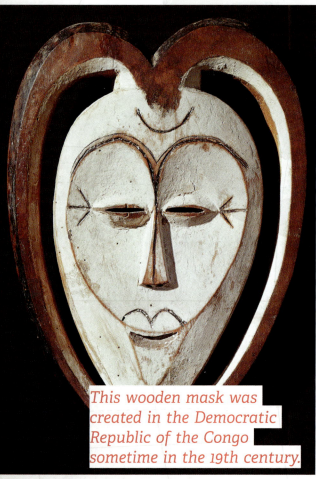

This wooden mask was created in the Democratic Republic of the Congo sometime in the 19th century.

People wear sacred masks during a ceremony in Côte d'Ivoire, Africa, in 2019.

CULTURAL CONNECTIONS

Some people think of masks as an art form common to all of Africa. However, they're not part of the **heritage** of all African peoples, and groups that do use masks don't always use them in the same ways.

Wood carving isn't limited to just the making of masks, however. It's a popular and common form of art for many peoples of Africa, as are pottery, painting, and jewelry making. Some peoples, including the Nupe and Yoruba of Nigeria and the Senufo of Côte d'Ivoire, make intricately carved wooden doors. Painting can also mean decorating buildings, including **murals** created by the Nuba and Burun peoples of Sudan and South Sudan.

A man takes a photo in front of a mural in Sudan in 2019.

mural: A painting on a ceiling or wall, often in a public place.

Contemporary African Visual Artists

The artistic traditions of sub-Saharan Africa continue today. Artists use both traditional and modern forms of materials and expression, creating works with a diversity of themes. Chéri Samba of the Democratic Republic of Congo is a painter who showcases his perception of daily life in Africa. Sokari Douglas Camp of Nigeria is a sculptor who works mainly with steel, inspired by Kalabari culture. Abdoulaye Konaté works in textiles, including materials from his native Mali. Ibrahim El-Salahi of Sudan is a painter sometimes considered the godfather of African **modernism**. He's been painting and creating art for more than 50 years.

Chéri Samba's painting J'aime la couleur is shown on display in London, England, in 2019.

Sculptor Sokari Douglas Camp is shown with one of her sculptures in 2003.

modernism: A style of art or literature that uses ideas or ways that are very different from past ways.

CULTURAL CONNECTIONS

Body decoration is another form of art for many African peoples. This may include body painting and tattoos.

Textile arts are among the most common forms of sub-Saharan African art known in the West. As with other forms of art, there's a huge variety in forms and materials. One well-known African textile is *adinkra* cloth, which is made by the Asante people of Ghana. Creators weave cloth from cotton or wool and then stamp designs (also called adinkra) on it. The Asante people and others also create kente cloth, another well-known textile. This

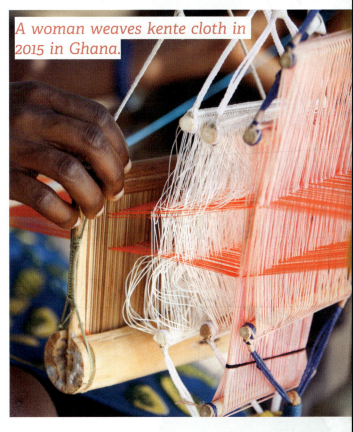

A woman weaves kente cloth in 2015 in Ghana.

textile: A kind of cloth that is woven or knit.

Clothing as Art

Pieces of clothing can be works of art. Like everything else, traditional clothing varies in sub-Saharan Africa. Most people wear Western-style clothing today, but some modern-day clothing has its roots in older dress. Some well-known fashions include the agbada, a loose-fitting robe worn by men in Nigeria and some other places; wraps and dresses made of ankara cloth, which has brightly colored patterns; boubous, robes worn in central and west Africa; geles, which are headdresses; and dashiki and *madiba* shirts.

cloth is woven from silk or cotton and often features bright colors and geometric stripes and bands. The Bamana people of Mali make *bogolan* cloth. Strips of cotton fabric are dyed and printed with a kind of **fermented** mud.

5 MUSIC, DANCE, AND STORIES

The arts of music, dance, and theater are a very important part of African culture. Aspects of the three art forms are often woven together into a whole. As with visual arts such as sculpture and painting, they can have both ceremonial and entertainment functions in both traditional and modern society. They may also have religious functions, serving as interactions with spiritual forces. They may even be a form of **therapy** and education. There are work songs as well, performed while people are working together.

Common musical styles and instruments differ from place to place, but there are some common threads. Percussion is very important

---

therapy: A way of dealing with problems that makes people's bodies and minds feel better.

Dancers and musicians (on djembe drums and other instruments) perform in Burundi in 2015.

in sub-Saharan African music, and drums often play key parts in ceremonies. While there are many different types of drums, one of the most well-known and often-used is the *djembe*, a drum often carved from a single piece of wood and topped with a stretched piece of animal skin. This type of drum, which has roots in west Africa, has been used for hundreds of years.

CULTURAL CONNECTIONS

Popular music styles in Africa include west Africa's highlife and juju, east Africa's *tarabu*, and South Africa's *chimurenga* and *jit* music.

Other Instruments

While drums are very important to African music, there are other notable traditional instruments as well. Percussion instruments include the mbira (an instrument whose sound is made by plucking pieces of metal or other materials), rattles such as maracas or *shekere*, bells, and xylophones such as the marimba. There are also string instruments, such as the musical bow and types of harps and lutes, including the 21-stringed kora harp. Wind instruments include flutes, whistles, trumpets, and clarinets.

Musicians play the kora at the 2016 funeral of M'Bady Kouyate, a griot from Guinea.

Members of the Maasai people perform an adumu dance during a coming-of-age ritual in Tanzania.

The rhythmic motions of African dance range from quite simple to very complex. Dances often express emotion and are used for specific events. For example, the *adumu* dance of the Maasai people of Kenya is part of the coming-of-age ceremony for young men. In it, each dancer tries to jump higher than the others. Dances also sometimes take place during funeral rites. The *igogo* dance of the Owo-Yoruba people features stamping steps to pack the earth into place over a grave.

CULTURAL CONNECTIONS

Enslaved people stolen from sub-Saharan Africa often continued their musical traditions in the Americas. In call-and-response music, a chorus responds to a lead singer. Gospel, blues, and rock and roll were influenced by this style, which originated in west Africa.

Ancient Sounds

Records of African music and dance—in the form of rock paintings showing dance scenes—date back as far as 5000 BC. There are dance styles shown in this art form that resemble dances still performed today. Other pictures of musical instruments, including drums and bells, have been found painted on **artifacts** in present-day Benin, Nigeria, and other locations. By the 14th century, there are written accounts of African music from Arab and European travelers. **Migrations** by African peoples brought musical styles and instruments from one location on the continent to others.

Ancient rock art, such as this scene from the Tassili-n-Ajjer plateau of Algeria, gives us a glimpse into daily life in ancient Africa. Some other rock paintings showed dancers, indicating ancient musical traditions that existed in both North Africa and sub-Saharan Africa.

artifact: Something made by humans in the past that still exists.
migration: Movement from one region to another.

CULTURAL CONNECTIONS

Femi Osofisan of Nigeria is another prominent African playwright. His plays, which include *Once Upon Four Robbers*, have been produced in Nigeria, Ghana, Great Britain, and the United States.

Traditional African theater is often woven into practices of dance and music. Performances take place right out in the community, rather than in specific places, and can tell stories and be part of rituals.

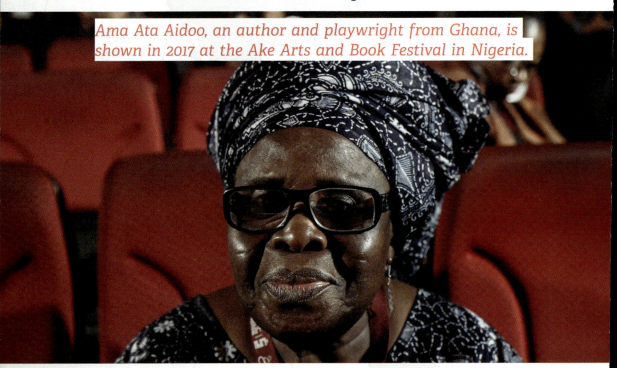

Ama Ata Aidoo, an author and playwright from Ghana, is shown in 2017 at the Ake Arts and Book Festival in Nigeria.

Griots and other storytellers often use questions and answers to include the audience. After the colonial era, around the middle of the 20th century, different forms of theater emerged, many of them criticizing colonialism and looking toward independence. One famous playwright, Ama Ata Aidoo of Ghana, wrote *The Dilemma of a Ghost* (1965) and *Anowa* (1970). Both plays explore history and the legacy of slavery.

Girls sing and chant during a street carnival celebrating Africa Month in Durban, South Africa.

6
CHALLENGES, VICTORIES, AND LIFE

Life in sub-Saharan Africa isn't without its challenges. In addition to the infrastructure issues in some areas, some regions deal with extreme poverty. In fact, more than half of people classified as extremely poor (living on less than $2 a day) live in sub-Saharan Africa. This poverty is concentrated in nine countries: Nigeria, the Democratic Republic of the Congo, Ethiopia, Tanzania, Madagascar, Kenya, Mozambique, Uganda, and Malawi. This isn't always a question of the country's overall wealth, but rather of the distribution of resources.

However, many countries are working to reduce these issues—and having some success. Tanzania reduced its extreme poverty rate from 86 percent in 2000 to 49 percent in 2015. Additionally, half of the 12 fastest-growing economies in the world are in Africa, and its potential workforce and middle class are growing quickly. Most people in Africa live somewhere between wealth and poverty, just like people in many other areas.

> **CULTURAL CONNECTIONS**
>
> In 2018, the majority of people in the sub-Saharan African countries of South Africa, Ghana, Senegal, Nigeria, Kenya, and Tanzania owned a mobile phone.

There have also been issues with violence and war in sub-Saharan Africa. Conflict has arisen over resources and religions, and the area has also seen **ethnic conflict** and **genocide**. The region has more than

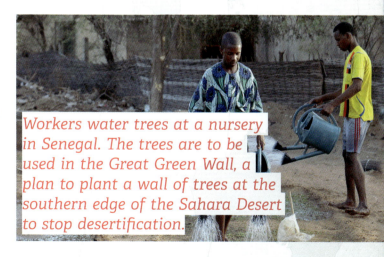

Workers water trees at a nursery in Senegal. The trees are to be used in the Great Green Wall, a plan to plant a wall of trees at the southern edge of the Sahara Desert to stop desertification.

ethnic conflict: Tension between two groups with different ethnicities.
genocide: Systematic killing of a particular ethnic group.

26 percent of the world's refugee population, putting further stress on sometimes-strained resources. Climate change has also taken a toll, with **droughts**, desertification, and natural disasters, such as earthquakes and flooding.

Nollywood and the Film Industry

The term "Nollywood" refers to Nigeria's growing film industry, which makes more than 1,500 movies a year. It's now the second-largest film industry worldwide in terms of movies made, second only to India's Bollywood, and its movies are available around the world, including on YouTube and streaming services like Netflix. In October 2019, there were 10 African films submitted to the Academy Awards' International Feature Film category—more than ever before. Entries came from Ghana, Senegal, and Nigeria. Only three African films have won the award so far, however. The last one was *Tsotsi* from South Africa, which won the category in 2006.

Customers look at Nollywood movies at a shop in Lagos, Nigeria.

drought: A long period of very dry weather.

However, Africa, as a whole, isn't an unsafe place. In fact, many places are considered safer and more peaceful than areas of the United States. As a whole, in 2019, the Global Peace Index considered sub-Saharan Africa more peaceful than Russia and Eurasia, South Asia, and the Middle East and North Africa. Contrary to what some people in the West believe, there are also diverse climates and weather patterns in different regions of Africa. There are deserts, but some places are very green and lush.

Many people in Western countries have a mental image of Africans living side by side with large wild animals such as lions—but most Africans have never seen these animals except in pictures, just like most Americans. This lioness is in a reserve in Kenya.

CULTURAL CONNECTIONS

Football (called soccer in the United States) is the most popular sport in Africa. In 2010, South Africa became the first African nation to host the soccer World Cup.

Cuisine of Africa

The cuisine, or food, of sub-Saharan Africa is as diverse as everything else about the region. *Fufu* is a staple dish of west and central Africa. It's made of starchy ingredients such as yams and plantains (a fruit) that have been pounded into a dough with water. There are many different kinds, and people often eat them with stews or soups, which are also very popular in the region. Injera is a sort of flatbread from Ethiopian cuisine that's made from the grain teff. In southern Africa in particular, barbecued meat (*braai*) is very popular. It's often served with pap, a sort of porridge.

Men cook grilled meat in 2019 in Côte d'Ivoire.

The people of sub-Saharan Africa have rich cultures that blend traditional ways of life with modern ways. They excel at art, music, oral storytelling, and literature, and face challenges with new technology and ideas. This diversity of experience makes life in sub-Saharan Africa unique and an important part of the wider world.

Soccer City Stadium in Johannesburg, South Africa, is lit up before the 2010 World Cup final, the first held in Africa.

A boy holds up a Nigeria scarf during a Women's World Cup soccer match between Nigeria and Germany in 2019.

GLOSSARY

aesthetic: Related to art or beauty.

amulet: A small item worn to protect the owner against bad things.

climate change: Long-term change in Earth's climate, caused primarily by human activities such as burning oil and natural gas.

fermented: Having gone through a chemical change that may result in alcohol.

hereditary: Passed from parent to child, or from one generation to the next.

heritage: The traditions and beliefs that are part of the history of a group or nation.

initiation: A ceremony or series of actions that make a person part of a group.

intricate: Highly detailed and complex.

missionary: Someone who travels to a new place to spread their faith.

monolithic: Relating to something very large, tall, and narrow.

nomadic: Having to do with people who move from place to place.

oral: Spoken instead of written.

sustainable: Able to be maintained at a certain level or rate.

urbanize: To make more urban, or like a city; to form towns and cities and make them larger and more modern.

FOR MORE INFORMATION

BOOKS:

Atinuke. *Africa, Amazing Africa: Country by Country*. London, UK: Walker Books, 2019.

Gifford, Clive. *Not for Parents! Africa: Everything You Ever Wanted to Know*. Footscray, Victoria: Lonely Planet, 2013.

Koontz, Robin Michal. *Learning About Africa*. Minneapolis, MN: Lerner Publications, 2016.

WEBSITES:

Africa Facts
www.ducksters.com/geography/africa.php
Learn more about Africa's geography, how it looks on a map, and which countries make up the region.

South Africa Facts
www.natgeokids.com/za/discover/geography/countries/facts-about-south-africa/
National Geographic's website offers facts, maps, photographs, and more about this country in sub-Saharan Africa.

Top 20 Africa Facts
www.kids-world-travel-guide.com/africa-facts.html
This website features 20 fascinating facts about Africa and links to explore further.

Publisher's note to educators and parents: Our editors have carefully reviewed these websites to ensure that they are suitable for students. Many websites change frequently, however, and we cannot guarantee that a site's future contents will continue to meet our high standards of quality and educational value. Be advised that students should be closely supervised whenever they access the internet.

INDEX

A

Algeria 37
Angola 7, 9, 15
art 27, 29, 30, 31, 32, 37, 45

B

Benin 7, 9, 15, 37
Botswana 7, 9
Burundi 7, 34

C

Cape Verde 7, 15
Congo, Democratic Republic of the 7, 10, 28, 30, 40
Côte d'Ivoire 7, 16, 26, 28, 29

E

Ethiopia 7, 8, 10, 12, 19, 22, 23, 40, 44

G

Ghana 7, 15, 31, 38, 39, 41, 42

griot 16, 17, 35, 39
Guinea 7, 35

K

Kenya 7, 18, 24, 36, 40, 41

L

language 5, 13, 14, 15, 16, 19
literature 15, 16, 18, 19, 45

M

Madagascar 7, 15, 40
Malawi 7, 40
Mali 7, 8, 9, 19, 30, 32
Mauritania 7, 9
Mozambique 7, 40
music 16, 33, 34, 35, 36, 37, 38, 45

N

Namibia 7, 9
Niger 7, 9

Nigeria 7, 9, 10, 11, 13, 15, 18, 24, 29, 30, 32, 37, 38, 40, 41, 42, 45

S

Senegal 7, 41, 42
South Africa 7, 14, 16, 17, 18, 39, 41, 42, 43, 45
South Sudan 7, 20, 29
Sudan 29, 30

T

Tanzania 5, 7, 36, 40, 41
technology 10, 12, 45
Togo 7, 9

U

Uganda 7, 40

Z

Zambia 7
Zimbabwe 7, 19